THE OGS LEARN TO FLY

Felicity Everett

Designed by Maria Wheatley
and Graham Round

Illustrated by Graham Round

Language and Reading Consultant: David Wray
(Education Department, University of Exeter, England)

Series Editor: Gaby Waters

First published in 1995 by Usborne Publishing Ltd, Usborne House, 83-85 Saffron Hill, London EC1N 8RT, England.
Printed in Portugal. UE. First published in America August 1995.

The Ogs lived long ago
near a place called Ogtown.

Their home was a cave.
It was damp and chilly,
but the Ogs loved it.

Especially at bedtime,
when it seemed almost snug.

One night, the Ogs were sound asleep, when their peace was shattered...
CRASH RUMBLE RUMBLE RUMBLE
...by a terrible noise.
The Ogs woke up, terrified.
What on earth is that?
Is it T. Rex?
Or the end of the world?

What did Bruno think had happened?

The Ogs peeped out of the cave.
They couldn't see T. Rex. And it didn't look as though the world had ended just yet.
So they set off for Ogtown to see if anyone else had heard the hullaballoo.

They hadn't gone very far when...
YIKES! Who moved the path?
DANGER
EARTHQUAKE
ZONE
Of course no one had moved the path.
Can you guess what had really happened?

The terrible
noise was
an earthquake.

Yesterday there had been
a path through the woods.
Today there was a
huge crevasse.

And to make
matters worse,
the Ogs were
on one side of it.

And Ogtown was
on the other.

OGTOWN
Oh no!
We may never see Ogtown again.
That would be terrible.
Test today!
TOWN SCHOOL
ROCKY
FERN
CLIFF
ZOG
MOG
Mog didn't seem too bothered. Why not?

Here's what we'll do.
Ma was always good in a crisis.
The Ogs went home, split into pairs and put on their Thinking Caps.
A.B.C.
TRAMPOLINE

Each pair tried to think of a way to cross the crevasse and reach Ogtown.

Bruno's job was to look things up, but he was having a problem.

Can you see why?

That afternoon, the Ogs went back to the crevasse to put their plans into action.
First Ma and Pa tried out their homemade lasso.
It was looking good...
...until Pa let go of the rope.

Next Mog launched Grandpa
Good luck.
from a giant catapult.
But the elastic was gone
in Grandpa's long johns
and he fell,
SPLOSH
in the mud.
Can you see where
his glasses ended up?

Now it was down to
Zog and Grandma.
Grandma had
spent hours knitting
the trampoline.
Now everyone
just prayed it
would work.
ZOG
I can't bear
to look.
Zog bounced once, twice, three times.

Then he soared up, up and away.

Oh dear!
Zog had left
something behind.

Can you see what it was?

Poor Zog was just a hairsbreadth short of the other side.
Heeelp. My baby!
Luckily a passing pteranodon swooped down and rescued him in the nick of time.

The pteranodon blushed.

But there *was* a problem that no one had spotted.

Can you see what it was?

The pteranodon took a running jump,

flapped her wings like mad...

...and nose dived into a tree.

NO MORE THAN FIVE PASSENGERS
No wonder we crashed!
We were too heavy for her.
Where am I?
She's in no state to fly anywhere now.
Whatever shall we do?
But Grandpa was looking at the pteranodon with a strange smile on his face.
I think I feel an invention coming on. To the cave!

Grandpa disappeared inside the cave.

All day, mysterious noises could be heard.

Then, just when the other Ogs thought they'd die of curiosity, Grandpa came out.

He was inside the strangest thing the Ogs had ever seen.

It was a flying machine.

Grandpa had given it a name.
Can you see what it was?

The Ogs climbed nervously aboard.

Grandpa pulled a lever,
cranked a handle
and with a shudder
and a hum,

they were airborne.

Orville sailed over the crevasse and, in next to no time, they were landing in Ogtown market square.

It caused quite a stir.

One market boy wasn't very pleased.

What was his name?

There was no doubt about it, Orville had changed the Ogs' lives forever.

And someone else's too.